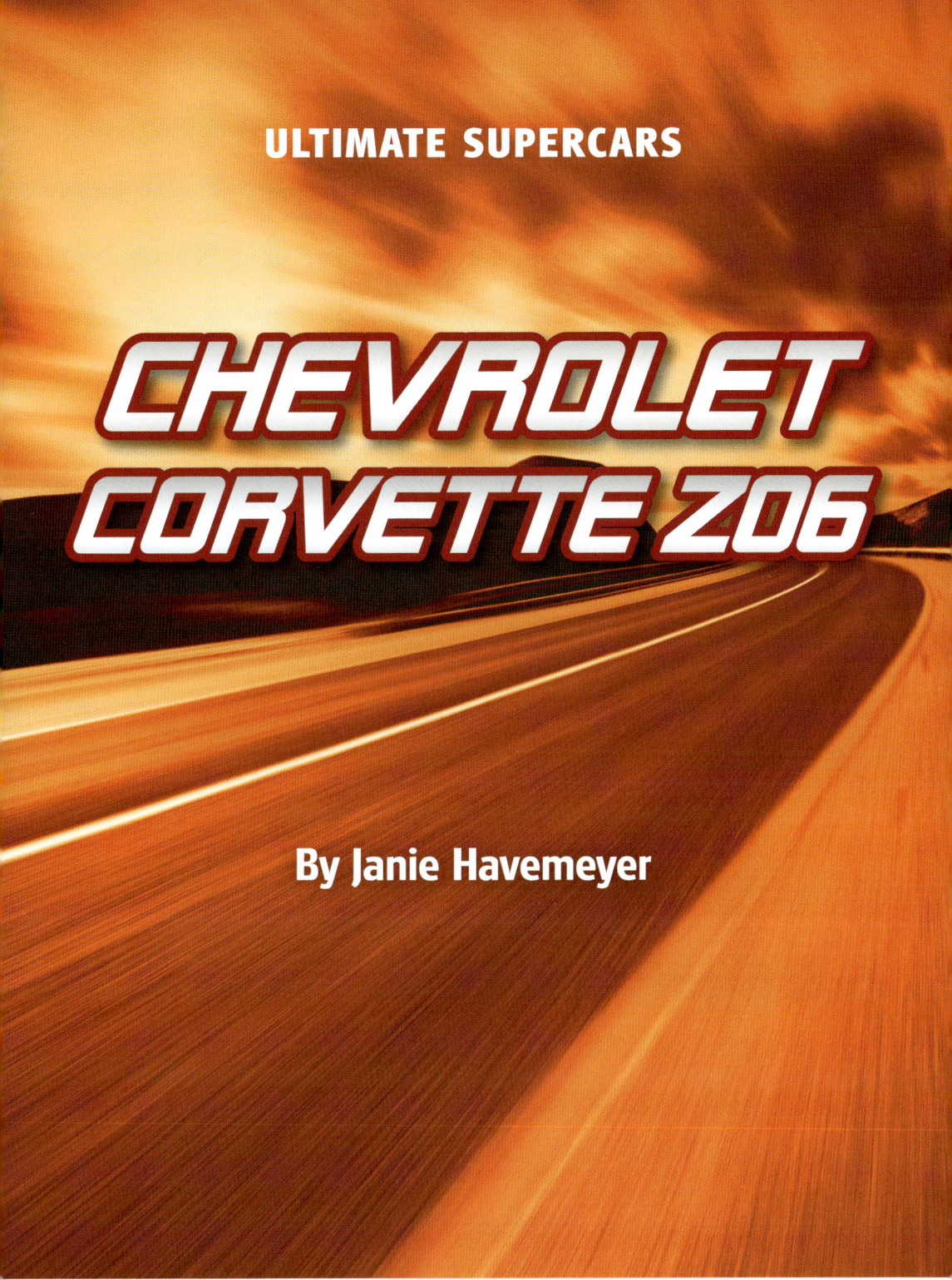

ULTIMATE SUPERCARS

CHEVROLET CORVETTE Z06

By Janie Havemeyer

Kaleidoscope
Minneapolis, MN

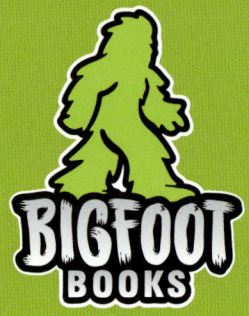

The Quest for Discovery Never Ends

This edition is co-published by agreement between Kaleidoscope and World Book, Inc.

Kaleidoscope Publishing, Inc.
6012 Blue Circle Drive
Minnetonka, MN 55343 U.S.A.

World Book, Inc.
180 North LaSalle St., Suite 900
Chicago IL 60601 U.S.A.

All rights reserved. No part of this book may be reproduced in any form without written permission from the publishers.

Kaleidoscope ISBNs
978-1-64519-026-4 (library bound)
978-1-64494-233-8 (paperback)
978-1-64519-126-1 (ebook)

World Book ISBN
978-0-7166-4327-2 (library bound)

Library of Congress Control Number
2019940222

Text copyright ©2020 by Kaleidoscope Publishing, Inc. All-Star Sports, Bigfoot Books, and associated logos are trademarks and/or registered trademarks of Kaleidoscope Publishing, Inc.

Printed in the United States of America.

Bigfoot lurks within one of the images in this book. It's up to you to find him!

TABLE OF
CONTENTS

Chapter 1: Driving the Corvette Z06 4

Chapter 2: History of the Z06 10

Chapter 3: At the Car Show 16

Chapter 4: A Museum-Worthy Car 22

Beyond the Book 28
Research Ninja 29
Further Resources 30
Glossary 31
Index 32
Photo Credits 32
About the Author 32

CHAPTER 1

DRIVING THE CORVETTE Z06

Jim Mero presses down hard on the gas pedal. The engine roars. He is driving the Chevrolet Corvette Z06. He takes his left foot off the brake. The car shoots across the starting line. It leaves behind a plume of smoke. The Z06 reaches 60 miles per hour (97 km/h) in three seconds. Mero reaches the first bend in the track. It is shaped like a horseshoe. The tires grip the road. The Z06 rounds the corner. It speeds up.

The Corvette Z06 can go from 0–60 miles per hour (97 km/h) in three seconds.

Mero is a test driver. He is racing on a track in Virginia. The event is called the Lightning Lap competition. New cars compete to be the fastest every year. Cars drive one at a time. A timer records how fast a car completes the track. Mero has spent several days on the course. He practiced driving on it. It is winding and hilly. There are twenty-four sharp turns. Now the time has come to test the Z06.

Mero races up a hill. The Z06 goes faster. It hits 134 miles per hour (216 km/h). Mero shifts **gears** as he goes into turns. This helps him control his speed. He also uses his brakes. If he brakes too late, he might crash.

spoiler

air intakes

aluminum frame

PARTS OF A CORVETTE Z06

removable roof

FUN FACT
Z06 is pronounced "Z-Oh-Six."

Corvette logo

The track straightens out. The Z06 reaches 140 miles per hour (225 km/h). Mero grips the steering wheel. The car sounds like thunder. It zooms down the last stretch. It flies across the finish line. Then the timer stops. The Z06 has finished the race in 2 minutes and 44.6 seconds. It's a new record! It is the fastest new car on the market that year. The Z06 is named the winning **supercar** of 2015.

THE GRAND COURSE

The Grand Course is a race track. It's where the Lightning Lap competition takes place. It is one of America's hardest race courses. It's part of the Virginia International Raceway. Thousands of people come every year to watch races. The raceway is a popular place to test new cars.

The Z06 has four exhaust pipes.

CHAPTER 2

HISTORY OF THE Z06

Harley J. Earl paid attention to cars. He designed them for **General Motors**. It is a big American car company. General Motors owns Chevrolet. Earl noticed a new car on the road. The car was small. It had only two seats. It was called a sports car. Sports cars were made in Europe. Soldiers fighting in Europe brought them back to America. They were fun to drive. Earl decided to build an American sports car. He named it the Corvette. The first Chevrolet Corvette came out in 1953.

At first, Corvettes were not the best sports cars. They were too slow. But Earl did not give up. He hired Zora Arkus-Duntov. Arkus-Duntov was a race car driver. He worked on the engine. Soon the cars were selling well. Owners raced them against European sports cars. Now the Corvettes won.

FUN FACT
The first Z06 cost over $50,000 in today's money.

The first Corvette was released in 1953.

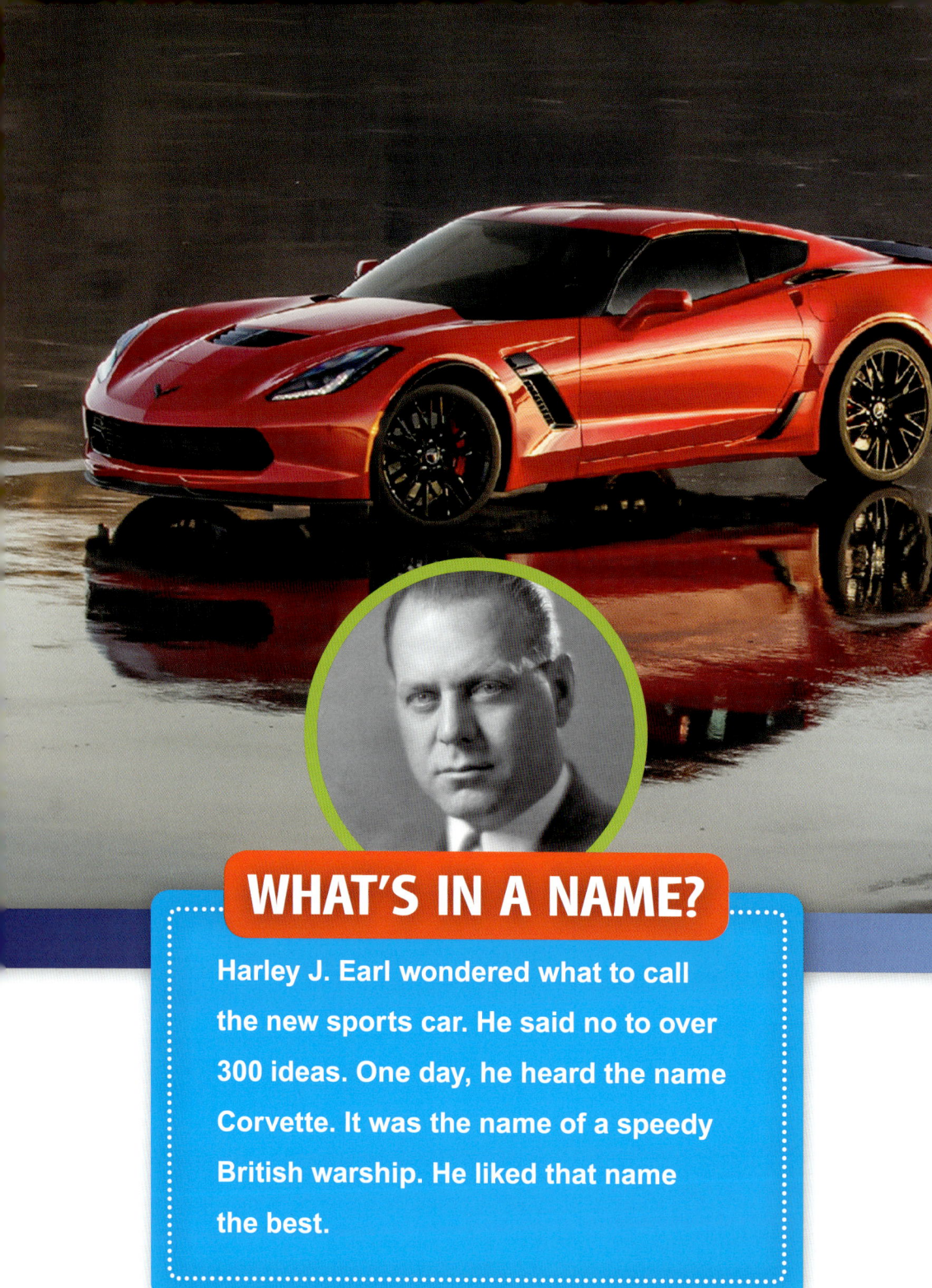

WHAT'S IN A NAME?

Harley J. Earl wondered what to call the new sports car. He said no to over 300 ideas. One day, he heard the name Corvette. It was the name of a speedy British warship. He liked that name the best.

The Corvette Z06 has changed a lot since 1963.

The Corvette Z06 came out in 1963. It was a special Corvette. It was meant for racing. It had a larger fuel tank than a regular Corvette. This meant drivers did not have to stop for gas as often. They could keep racing. The Z06 also had stronger brakes and better steering. It was lighter than the regular Corvette. Only 199 were built at first. People who owned one felt special.

The Z06 goes through small changes every year. But it has gone through several major changes since 1963. One was in 2004. It was built with larger tires. It had lighter parts. In 2013, it was built on a lighter frame. The frame was made out of aluminum. Another new model came out in 2015. Now it had a removable top. The new engine shocked the world. It was the most powerful engine yet.

The Z06's engines are built in Bowling Green, Kentucky.

Where the Corvette Z06 Is Made

1 **Detroit, Michigan:** Chevrolet Headquarters

2 **Bowling Green, Kentucky:** Where the Corvette Z06 is assembled and the engines are made

CHAPTER 3

AT THE CAR SHOW

A car engine roars. Lights dim in the showroom. The New York Auto Show is about to start. A Corvette Z06 rolls on stage. It's shiny and blue. It stops and spins on a turntable. Loud music blares. The crowd cheers. Cameras flash.

Mark Reuss steps out. He is the executive vice president of General Motors. "Ladies and gentlemen," he says. "Introducing the first ever supercar **convertible** from Chevrolet!" The crowd can't wait to hear more.

Mark Reuss introduced the 2015 Z06 at the New York Auto Show.

The Z06 comes in both manual and automatic transmission.

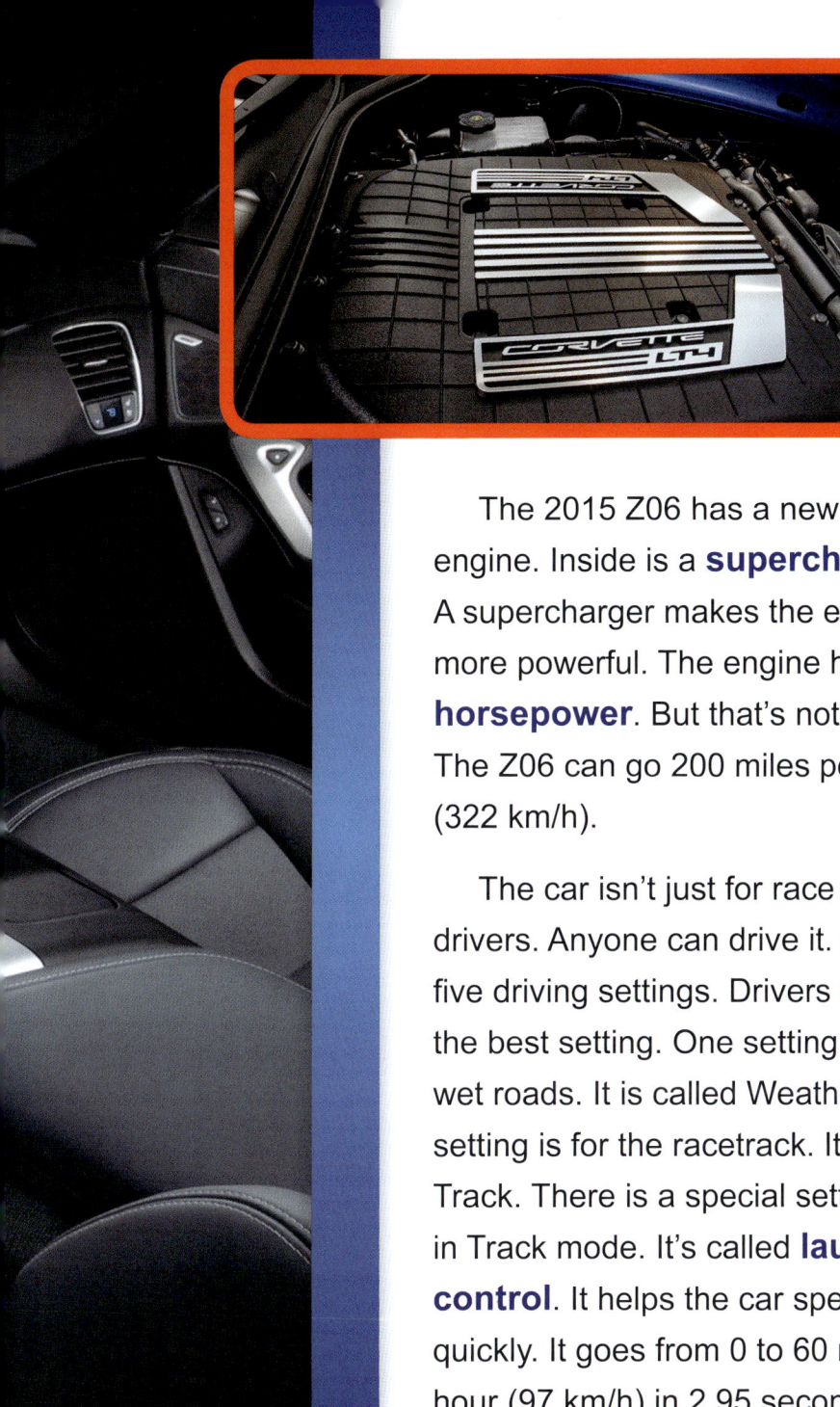

The 2015 Z06 has a new engine. Inside is a **supercharger**. A supercharger makes the engine more powerful. The engine has 625 **horsepower**. But that's not all. The Z06 can go 200 miles per hour (322 km/h).

The car isn't just for race car drivers. Anyone can drive it. It has five driving settings. Drivers choose the best setting. One setting is for wet roads. It is called Weather. One setting is for the racetrack. It is called Track. There is a special setting in Track mode. It's called **launch control**. It helps the car speed up quickly. It goes from 0 to 60 miles an hour (97 km/h) in 2.95 seconds. The Z06 has "won just about every race we competed in," Mr. Reuss says.

THE CORVETTE Z06
IN DETAIL

Height: 4.1 feet (1.2 m)

Width: 6.5 feet (2 m)

Length: 14.8 feet (4.5 m)

Weight: 3,770 pounds (1,710 kg)

Top Speed: 210 miles per hour (338 km/h)

Time from 0–60 miles per hour (0–97 km/h): 2.95 seconds

COST: $80,900 (2019 MODEL)

THE FLYING DENTIST

The Gulf One is the name of a famous Z06. Dick Thompson owned it. He was a dentist who started racing. He won many races in the 1950s and 1960s. People called him "the Flying Dentist." The Gulf One sold in 2009. It went for over $1 million.

The crowd likes what they hear next. The Z06 costs $79,000. The price is surprising. Other supercars cost twice as much. The supercar is made in a Corvette factory. It is built on an **assembly line**. This brings the cost down. The crowd cheers. The car spins one more time. Then it drives off.

FUN FACT
The Z06 was the first road car to run the Nürburgring course in Germany in under 8 minutes.

CHAPTER 4

A MUSEUM-WORTHY CAR

Sam likes it when his dad picks him up from school. He gets to ride in the Z06. Sam and his dad drive around with the top down. It's fun to ride in the open air. Sam's family loves Corvettes. There are thousands of fans like them.

The Corvette Z06 is a popular car.

They live all around the world. Sam even joined a club for kids who love Corvettes. It's called the Future Corvette Owners Association.

FUN FACT
There is a special driving school to learn how to drive the Z06.

Sam's family picked up their Z06 together. They wanted it to be a family event. They drove to Kentucky. They toured the Corvette factory. The National Corvette Museum is next door. They picked up the car there. Sam liked seeing the other cars in the museum. But the Z06 is his favorite. Their Z06 was on display. Sam's parents had customized it.

For an extra fee, Corvette buyers can pick up their cars at the Corvette Museum.

There were ten paint colors. They could choose the wheels. They picked yellow brake **calipers**. Sam loved seeing their car in the museum. It made him feel special. The Z06 is a popular car. A car magazine made a list of the ten best cars for 2019. The Z06 was on the list.

The Corvette museum has many **raffles**. Winners receive new cars. A 2019 winner won a Z06. Sam will be old enough to drive in eight years. He hopes to win a Z06 too.

In 2014, a sinkhole opened up under the Corvette Museum, damaging eight cars. Three have been restored, and the other five are on display as-is to memorialize the event.

The Corvette has a long history.

    The Corvette Z06 is a classic sports car. It has been around for fifty years. Sam hopes it will be around for more. He can't wait to see what the future holds.

BEYOND
THE BOOK

After reading the book, it's time to think about what you learned. Try the following exercises to jumpstart your ideas.

THINK

THAT'S NEWS TO ME. Jim Mero raced the Z06 at a racetrack. He broke a track record. How might news sources be able to fill in more detail about this? What new information could you find in news articles? Where could you go to find those sources?

CREATE

PRIMARY SOURCES. A primary source is an original document, photograph, or interview. Make a list of different primary sources you might be able to find about the Corvette Z06. What new information might you learn from these sources?

SHARE

SUM IT UP. Write one paragraph summarizing the important points from this book. Make sure it's in your own words. Don't just copy what is in the text. Share the paragraph with a classmate. Does your classmate have any comments about the summary? Do they have additional questions about the Corvette Z06?

GROW

REAL-LIFE RESEARCH. What places could you visit to learn more about the Corvette Z06? What other things could you learn while you were there?

RESEARCH NINJA

Visit www.ninjaresearcher.com/0264 to learn how to take your research skills and book report writing to the next level!

RESEARCH

DIGITAL LITERACY TOOLS

SEARCH LIKE A PRO
Learn about how to use search engines to find useful websites.

FACT OR FAKE?
Discover how you can tell a trusted website from an untrustworthy resource.

TEXT DETECTIVE
Explore how to zero in on the information you need most.

SHOW YOUR WORK
Research responsibly—learn how to cite sources.

WRITE

GET TO THE POINT
Learn how to express your main ideas.

PLAN OF ATTACK
Learn prewriting exercises and create an outline.

DOWNLOADABLE REPORT FORMS

FURTHER RESOURCES

BOOKS

Cruz, Calvin. *Chevrolet Corvette Z06*. Bellwether Media, 2016.

Kingston, Seth. *The History of Corvettes*. PowerKids Press, 2019.

Murray, Julie. *Chevrolet Corvette*. Abdo Publishing, 2018.

WEBSITES

Factsurfer.com gives you a safe, fun way to find more information.

1. Go to www.factsurfer.com.
2. Enter "Chevrolet Corvette Z06" into the search box and click 🔍.
3. Select your book cover to see a list of related websites.

GLOSSARY

assembly line: An assembly line is a way of putting together a product by moving it along a line of workers. Each worker on the assembly line adds or adjusts a part until it is finished.

calipers: Calipers are part of a car's brake system. The calipers squeeze the brake pads to slow or stop a car.

convertible: A convertible is a car with a folding or soft roof. The 2015 Z06 was the first supercar convertible from Chevrolet.

gears: Gears help a car drive at different speeds. Mero shifted gears to go as fast as possible.

General Motors: General Motors is one of the three big US car makers. General Motors owns Buick, Cadillac, GMC, and Chevrolet.

horsepower: One horsepower is the power it takes to lift 550 pounds one foot in one second. The Z06 has 650 horsepower.

launch control: Launch control helps the car speed up quickly. Using launch control, the Corvette Z06 can go from 0 to 60 miles per hour (97 km/h) in 2.95 seconds.

raffles: Raffles are contests in which a ticket is chosen at random and the winner gets a prize. The Corvette Museum holds raffles every year for a new car.

supercar: A supercar is a very expensive, fast, or powerful car. The Corvette Z06 is a supercar made by Chevrolet.

supercharger: A supercharger is a part that increases an engine's power by pulling more air into the engine. A supercharger gives more power than a natural engine.

INDEX

Arkus-Duntov, Zora, 11

brakes, 4, 6, 13, 25

car show, 16–21

Corvette Museum, 24–26

cost, 11, 20, 21

Earl, Harley J., 10–11, 12

engine, 11, 14, 19

Flying Dentist, the, 21

Future Corvette Owners Association, 23

General Motors, 10, 17

horsepower, 19

launch control, 19

Lightning Lap competition, 4–8

Mero, Jim, 4–8

racetrack, 4–8, 19, 21

record, 8, 21

Reuss, Mark, 17–19

size, 20

steering, 4–6, 13

superchargers, 19

top speed, 20

PHOTO CREDITS

The images in this book are reproduced through the courtesy of: Chevrolet Media, front cover, pp. 4–5, 6–7, 8–9, 10–11, 12–13, 14, 18–19, 19, 22–23, 27, 30; Darren Brode/Shutterstock Images, p. 3; Steve Lagreca/Shutterstock Images, p. 9; GM Media Archives, p. 12; Red Line Editorial, p. 15; Mark Lennihan/AP Images, pp. 16–17; Steve Lagreca/Shutterstock Images, p. 20; Markus Volk/iStockphoto, p. 21; James R. Martin/Shutterstock Images, p. 24; Roman Korotkov/Shutterstock Images, pp. 24–25; Michael Noble Jr./AP Images, p. 26.

ABOUT THE AUTHOR

Janie Havemeyer is an author of many books for children. Janie loves learning about new topics. She is a graduate of Middlebury College and Bank Street Graduate School of Education. She lives in San Francisco, California.